MW01601522

GHOSTS *of the*

1000 ISLANDS

area of the St. Lawrence River

© Larry Hillhouse 2009

In order to meet the official guidelines for consideration as one of the islands making up the Thousand Islands, an island has to be above water for 365 days out of the year, and the island must support at least two living trees. Ghosts, however, aren't limited by any such rules, and thus their faction easily outnumbers the islands.

This book is dedicated to the many people who simply enjoy their reading with a bit of spookiness, to the people who have witnessed firsthand a ghostly sighting, and to the hordes of others who fervently desire to see one of these ghostly visions. To the first group, read on. To the second group, don't be afraid to tell your story. To the third group, be very careful what you wish for!

TABLE OF CONTENTS

PREFACE

The Thousand Islands Region has many qualifications to be inhabited with ghostly spirits. It has been home for hundreds of years to early Indian tribes and their many legends to explain everything in their surroundings. Then came the numerous explorers and settlers who clashed with the Indians, each other, and the environment. Wars, shipwrecks, marauding pirates, drownings, lost lovers, smuggling, gambling, other evils of society, castles, burned mansions, and personal tragedies all contributed to an atmosphere ripe for hauntings of many types. By all rights, this area should be literally overrun with ghostly beings. As a matter of fact, according to stories in this book, it is.

FOREWORD

The stories in this book are set along the St. Lawrence River, or Seaway, in an area known as the Thousand Islands Region. The St. Lawrence Seaway is one of the larger rivers of the world, covering some 775 miles.

Fifteen miles wide at its source, it tapers down to five miles in places and is sprinkled with the many islands. Flowing from the fresh water of the Great Lakes toward the salty Atlantic Ocean, it provides navigation directly into the heart of North America. It has been used for hundreds of years by the Aboriginal people, early explorers, trappers, and others for various personal and commercial applications.

It is an area proud of its extensive history, proven by the large number of museums and preserved historical sites along the river. It is also a popular attraction to the outdoor enthusiasts, providing canoeing, kayaking, fishing, and other exciting water sports activities.

Centuries ago there was an ancient mountain chain running along the current border of the United States and Canada. What later became known as the St. Lawrence River overran its banks and attempted to swallow these mountains, and almost succeeded. What remained were the tops of the higher mountains, forming hundreds of small islands. These islands run from Kingston past Brockville,  Ontario, on the Canadian side, joining the Canadian Shield and the Adirondack Mountains of New York State. On the American side the area runs from Oswego to Massena. Taking its name from the multitude of islands, the Thousand Islands Region includes both sides of the St. Lawrence River and the eastern shores of Lake Ontario.

There are actually over 1,800 official islands along the fifty mile span between Kingston and Brockville. Although some of them are simply rocky shoals, others are quite large. Wolfe Island is about twenty miles long and one to seven miles wide, and Howe Island is nearly nine miles long by three miles wide. To meet the official criteria to be one of the islands making up the chain, an island has to be above water for 365 days out of the year, and the island must support at least two living trees.

The islands have many diverse features, such as granite cliffs, sandy bays, dark pines, and pretty maple trees. There is enough variety to satisfy anyone's definition of scenic beauty.

The islands were originally deeded from the Indians to the Canadian and American governments. A boundary agreement made between Canada and the United States decreed that no island would be split in two, and the boundary should be at least one hundred yards from any shore. In the event that wasn't possible, the line would run right down the middle between the two shores. That resulted in the zigzag line that makes up the boundary between the two countries. Although about two thirds of the islands are in Canadian territory, the land acreage is close to equal between Canada and the United States. First the islands were popular primarily for their lumber and fur trade. Their abundant trees made the area the home of a major shipbuilding industry of both lake

schooners and ocean-worthy vessels.

Then as water sports, hunting, and vacation homes became trendy, the islands turned into a playground for the rich. Many of the islands were purchased by individuals for personal use, and have remained in the same families for generations. Vacationers discovered the islands in the late 1800s, and they became a fashionable summer retreat. Hotels, as well as private homes, sprang up all over the islands.

During this era, extravagant houses and mansions were built in the region. The famous Boldt Castle, built by George Boldt, the owner of the Waldorf Astoria Hotel in New York City, was one of the more prominent ones. Other well known names such as Pullman, Astor, and Rubenstein also built luxurious summer homes there.

The St. Lawrence Islands National Park, one of the smallest national parks in Canada, is nestled along the river, with hiking and bicycle paths to add to the water sports along the Thousand Islands Water Trail. Much of the land comprising the park was included in the original parcel sold to the Canadian government by the Mississauga Indians.

The tiny park consists of twenty-one granite islands and many islets, and its scenic beauty is grandly displayed from the Thousand Islands Parkway which overlooks the full length of the park. Although the majority of the islands in the park have docks, picnic facilities, and hiking trails, most can only be accessed by boat.

The park was established in 1914, preserving a rich ecological boundary in the area. Many species of plant life are found on these islands. Some islands within the park are the northernmost home to some of these plants, and some islands are the southernmost location, giving the islands diverse species even from island to island.

The animal life also differs vastly in the area. Only the animals that don't hibernate during the winter are able to cross over the ice to reach the other islands. It seems that each island has its own particular animal species, depending on the size, access, and privacy of the location.

Squirrels, mice, deer, fox, and porcupines are common on the different islands, and even the black rat snake is found on some of them. A wide variety of birds help populate the islands, and the water  certainly contains plentiful fish species.

Also found abundantly throughout this region are stories of a slightly sinister nature. Known as folklore, legends, family secrets, or simply tall tales, some of these stories have been told for centuries, and others are as new as the mound of dirt on a fresh grave. It is up to the individual reader to decide for themselves whether to take these stories as amusing anecdotes, absolute truths, or simply events which have yet to be fully explained.

Many people refuse to believe in the possibility of supernatural beings and scoff at those who do. The fear of ridicule keeps many stories from being related by the participant. Thus, there are likely many more of these ghosts or apparitions supposedly encountered than ever get publicly mentioned.

With such numerous ghost stories in our culture, there are either a lot of these supernatural creatures around, or people thoroughly enjoy telling and listening to the spooky tales. Perhaps it is a little of both?

Almost all of us have either had a strange, hard-to-explain incident happen to us, or we know someone who has. Who knows what may be lurking around the next corner in your house, or even right behind you at this very minute?

Typical places for ghost-encountering in North America are houses, especially old and/or vacant houses, graveyards, and

hotels. Places where there were deaths, particularly unexpected or violent deaths are also good places for ghostly gatherings. These include battlefields, construction sites, highways, cliffs, hospitals, museums, and bodies of water. The Thousand Islands area has all of these potential assembling places for ghosts, and there are certainly numerous stories describing many strange encounters around that region. This book will visit a few of them.

THE LOST SON

Kingston lies at the junction of the St. Lawrence River and Lake Ontario. It holds the distinction of having been the first capital city of Canada. Now the fresh water  sailing capital of the world, it is also home to fantastic historic ship-wreck diving. The Fort Henry National Historic Site resides in Kingston, as well as a thriving arts and entertainment scene. While a popular tourist city with its many diverse forms of entertainment, it is also home to stories of an unusual nature. One of the oldest occurred on the outskirts of the city, over a hundred years ago.

For many years there has been an eerie story told concerning a house near Kingston. Back in the late 1800s there was a woman living in the house with her only son. The husband of the family had been killed in a hunting accident, leaving the woman to care for herself and their pre-teenage boy.

One dark night during a snowstorm, the boy took a lantern and went out to make certain that the animals

were in the barn and that the barn door was securely fastened. The mother was busy preparing their evening meal, and didn't immediately notice that the boy had not returned as promptly as he should have. After waiting for a while, the woman lit another lantern and went out to check on the youngster. Alas, the boy was nowhere to be found. The animals were secure in the barn, but there was no sign of the young lad.

The panic-stricken mother continued to search until the snowstorm worsened to the point that she had to return to the house. At daylight, with still no sign of the son returning, the woman left again. She walked to a neighbor's house and told them of the situation, then resumed searching for her lost youngster.

That night, when the people assisting called off the search because of darkness, the mother went out again, alone with her lantern. She was never seen again. There was no sign of her or her lantern the following day. After a few weeks the people gave up on ever finding either the missing son or the mother. That's not the end of the story, however, as years later there is still reason to

believe that the mother's spirit has not given up the search.

Once or twice a year there is a strange light seen in the fields outside of Kingston. The light is most often observed around midnight, and it bobs along as if it comes from a lantern carried by a person walking slowly along. Nobody has ever been able to get close to the light, as it disappears whenever anyone approaches. Some local people claim to have seen the mystery light many times over the years.

Legend has it that the light is from the lantern carried by the ghost of the mother, who continues to search the area for her lost son. Or, some say it could be the ghost of the son still trying to find his way home.

THE SPIRITUAL BRIDGE

The Thousand Islands Parkway runs the length of the Thousand Islands National Park. Following the St. Lawrence River between Kingston and Brockville, the road provides a spectacular view along its route. Sometimes the view is more than just spectacular, according to many of the people who have traveled the Parkway after dusk.

Not long after the Thousand Islands Parkway was opened, there was a certain place along the road that began having more than its share of accidents.  The accidents almost exclusively occurred late at night. Gradually there was a pattern recognized concerning the wrecks.

Investigators were told that the drivers suddenly encountered an Indian on horseback standing in the middle of the road. Several accidents resulted in the people swerving off the road in order to avoid colliding with the horse and rider. After the vehicle came to a halt, there was never any sign of the horseman.

One bizarre thing was the investigators were never able to find any sign of hoof prints anywhere around the area where the horse was sighted. Then an even stranger event happened. A truck driver admitted that he was traveling above the speed limit, and did not have time to swerve from the imminent collision. Expecting a dramatic thud and possibly the horse and/or rider crashing

through his windshield, the driver was astounded as his truck passed right through the certain victims, as if they were thin air. In fact, he claimed that they did vanish into thin air, as he stopped his truck as soon as he could, and returned to the spot to look for them.

As this last story was widely told, other people came forward attesting to the fact that they, too, had seen the ghostly rider, but were afraid to say anything, certain that they would not be believed.

Since the incidents were numerous, and always occurred at the same spot in the road, someone did a little research on that location. What they discovered was that the road had been built across an ancient Indian burial ground. During the construction process, numerous bones and artifacts had been displaced.

Even though the objects had been returned to the ground close to their original resting place, the spirits apparently weren't happy. Perhaps there were more bones there than had been discovered.

Although most people refuse to believe that such a thing as an unhappy spirit exists, there were too many incidents at the location to ignore. At no little expense, a bridge was constructed over the spot, such that the traffic did not actually touch the possibly hallowed ground. Even though many people thought that it was a large expense spent foolishly, there has never been another accident or sighting at that spot on the Parkway.

THE PEG-LEG GHOST

The St. Lawrence has afforded a passageway from the sea for centuries. This passageway was as convenient for the bad guys as it was for the honest folk. There are many stories told of pirates sailing up the St. Lawrence to escape pursuit, and more interestingly, to hide treasure.

Ill-gotten bounty had to be stashed in a safe place. Otherwise the rightful owners or, perhaps even more likely, other pirates, might claim the treasure. One story often told involves a pirate leader by the name of Peg-leg Pete.

Back in the early 1700s there was a rash of pirate raids along the banks of the St. Lawrence River at current

Cornwall. The leader of these raids was Peg-leg Pete. One story was that he'd lost his right leg just above the knee while serving in the British Navy, a victim of a vicious battle in the Pacific. Sent home by the navy, an embittered and crippled Pete embarked on a life of crime. It began with petty thievery, then after stowing away on a commercial ship that was hijacked by pirates, Pete's life took a giant leap.

Pete was the only person spared on the ship, with the pirate captain having pity on Pete and taking him on as sort of an apprentice. Pete adapted quickly to the life of

a pirate, and soon had his own ship. Eventually Pete expanded to a four ship fleet, wreaking havoc on any ship passing in his vicinity.

Never a trusting person by nature, a characteristic enhanced by the companions conducive to his lifestyle, Pete began hiding treasure inland at what is now known as the Thousand Islands National Park.

After a few lucrative hauls on the high seas, Pete would sail up the St. Lawrence in relative obscurity, and then take the treasure and a couple of sailors in a small boat to one of the islands. There they would bury the treasure, but only after carefully drawing a map as to its location. Then legend has it that Pete would kill the sailors, throwing their bodies on top of the treasure, and then cover them with dirt. Supposedly he thought the ghosts of the dead men would guard the treasure.

Although Pete was thought to have buried treasure in the islands numerous times, he did not live to enjoy his booty. After one of his raids, his crew mutinied, took over the ship and the loot for themselves, and made Pete walk,  or in this case hop, the plank.

Over the years there have been many people claiming to have one of Pete's treasure maps. These maps have been sold, stolen, and shared for many years. There have been a number of people murdered because of these maps, and families have been split apart over the greed caused by the supposedly route to easy riches. As far as anyone officially knows, however, none of Pete's treasures have ever been recovered.

In the 1940s a man arrived at Lansdowne from the United States, claiming that he had an authentic map to one of Pete's treasures. Enlisting a local man as a guide, they embarked on a mission to a nearby island intending to recover the treasure. Although some of the landmarks described on the map were no longer present, they felt sure that they ascertained the exact location marked on the map.

In order to avoid anyone following them, the two men left in the middle of the night, confident that they were about to be rich men. The guide wandered up to a house near Fishers Landing the evening of the following day, babbling incoherently. He kept mentioning something about devils and pirates and ghosts. He refused to go back to where his partner had last been seen, but he gave directions to a search party.

The searchers reached the destination on the island the guide described, only to find the treasure hunter's body. There was a shovel stuck in the ground next to the

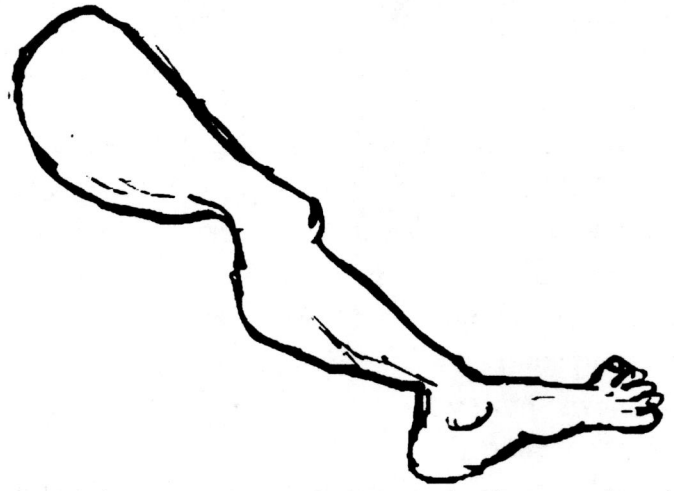

victim. The lone mark on the man's body was that his right leg had been severed just above the knee. There was no weapon or blood loss found anywhere around the area. The results of an autopsy could only suppose that the man had died of pure fright. Something scared him so bad that his heart simply stopped beating. Oh, and the man's severed leg was also never found.

THE GHOST MOURNER

During the 1930s a young couple from New York City settled in the town of Morristown, intent on making a new start with their life. According to rumors, the man had gotten into trouble with either the law or a gangster family, and the couple made a hasty exit from their previous home.

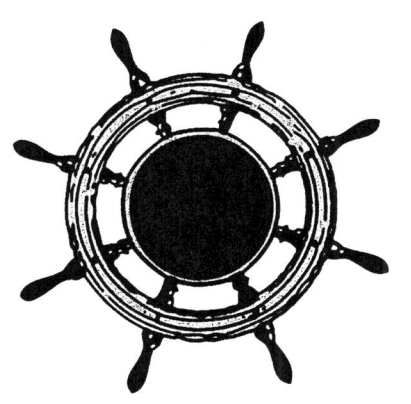

The husband soon found work on a fishing boat, and though the work was hard, seemed to have found a niche for himself. Alas, the peaceful life did not last for long, as the man was swept overboard and lost at sea during a sudden storm one day.

The young wife would be seen going to a church in the town early each morning, dressed in black. She would either kneel at the altar, or if anyone else was around, she would sit quietly on the back pew.

This was a ritual that was just like clockwork; she could be depended on to be at the church in the early hours each morning.

Within a year of the husband's death, the widow was found dead at the altar in the church. It was as if she had mourned herself to death. She was buried alongside her husband in the cemetery behind the church, and the people thought that would be the end of it, but it wasn't.

It was the church custodian who first saw the "woman in black" at the back of the church. The second time he saw her, he approached her, only to watch in astonishment as she disappeared into the wall.

Since then she has been seen many times in the church, usually by a person walking into what they thought was an empty sanctuary. Sometimes she is kneeling at the altar, and sometimes she is sitting or standing at the last pew in the back of the church. She is always dressed in a long black dress with a black veil hiding her face.

The lady has been seen by so many people that they simply accept the fact that their church has a resident mourning ghost. The widow apparently continues to grieve for her lost husband, and her ghost seeks comfort or some type of closure through her persistent visits to the church.

THE LEGEND OF THE MOSQUITO

It is a fact that some of the largest mosquitoes in North America can be found in the Thousand Islands area. These vicious little blood-suckers can be a real nuisance at times, and due to their long-standing habitat in the area, they have their very own Indian legend.

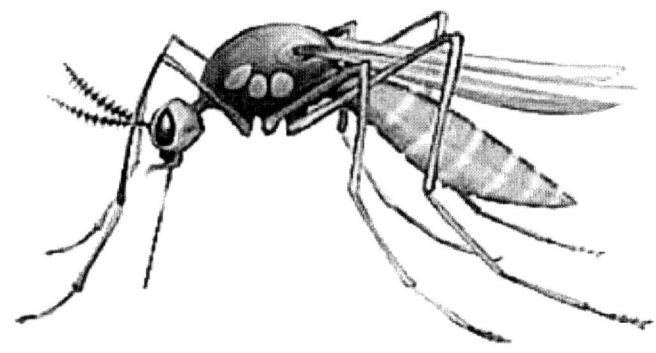

According to the legend, many years ago there was a hideous monster living in the dense forest on Wolfe Island. Whether measured by square miles or overall length, this is certainly the largest island in the chain. In the St. Lawrence River, and across from Kingston, this

Canadian island was originally very heavily wooded, providing ample cover for various animals and/or monsters.

This monster was seldom seen amidst the forests of the island except during the darkest of nights, when the moon was hidden by clouds. That was when the monster roamed about. The Indians thought that the monster was not an actual living creature, but more like a ghost of some devilish variety, born of evil, and destined to wreak havoc on all living creatures in the area.

At first the ghost monster was about the size of a normal man, except there wasn't much normal about the creature. It was half-man and half-beast. Although it walked on two legs  like a human, the feet were cloven hooves, the arms were longer than normal, the body was covered with long straggly hair, its head was more like that of a large wolf, its eyes were a glowing red color, and it had vicious fangs.

Over time, the monster grew larger, and was soon reported to be at least ten feet tall. The critter fed on blood. Carcasses of deer and smaller animals were frequently found by the Indians. Each time there would be puncture wounds on the victim's neck, and its blood would be totally drained from the body.

Unfortunately it wasn't just the animals that fell prey to the monster. It also seemed to like the blood of humans. An Indian brave or maiden venturing out alone on a dark night was a potential victim of the creature, their bloodless body discovered in the light of the following day.

Eventually the Indians grew weary of the fearful creature and decided that they had to do something. They sent for a medicine man from a different tribe.

This medicine man was reputed to have more mysterious powers than any other known. So with the aid of the magical man, they hatched a plan to rid themselves of the monster once and for all.

The next dark, cloudy night, a young Indian maiden appeared to sit alone on the bank of the island, tending a small campfire. Before long a dark, shadowy silhouette emerged from the edge of the forest.

Just as the creature approached the figure by the fire, twenty of the most accurate braves of the tribe quickly emerged from cover and shot arrows into the monster. The arrowheads had been dipped in a special poison concocted by the medicine man. This poison froze the fiend in its current form, paralyzing it briefly, and allowing time for the rest of the plan to be enacted.

As the monster paused in surprise and pain, the figure by the campfire jumped up and ran toward the ghost creature. It was the magical medicine man, and he threw a burning limb from the campfire onto the wounded critter. The limb was from a special tree, and had been empowered by a secret ceremony by the medicine man.

There was a large swoosh as fire completely engulfed the hairy monster. The creature howled a dreadful cry of agony, and then suddenly exploded into thousands of tiny pieces. These fragments of the blood-sucking monster became small blood-sucking flying insects. And, according to the Indian legend, that is where those pesky mosquitoes that still plague us today originated!

THE GHOST OF THE WEE PEOPLE

The village of Brockville was settled by an early group of Loyalist refugees displaced from their homes during the years of the American Revolution. An officer of one of the Loyalist regiments, William Buell, is considered to be the founder of Brockville.

There is a scenic pathway, the Brock Trail, running along Brockville's waterfront and through city parks. There are many plaques along the path, attesting to the historical past of the city. Also passing through the city is the Lake Ontario Waterfront Trail. The current residents are an out-going, friendly group, but are a far cry from some previous inhabitants.

When early explorers arrived in the area around what is now Brockville, they were amazed to find a small tribe of natives living there. Not that the tribe was small in number, but small in stature. None of the men were over three feet tall, and the women did not reach that height. Although perfectly proportioned otherwise, the people were simply a miniature tribe.

Supposedly the wee people, as the explorers called them, had certain Asian features which opened the possibility that their ancestors may have migrated from that part of the world.

Nevertheless, the wee people were friendly, although a bit shy. Once they were certain that the explorers meant them no harm, they mingled freely with them. The explorers, on the other hand, enjoyed having the small people around, and cultivated a friendship with them.

Then one day several boatloads of explorers from a French ship moved into the area. Thinking that the wee people were a freak of nature and worth a good price back in Europe, they proceeded to capture a large number of the small people, putting them in cages and transporting them back to their boats. A few of the wee people managed to escape and hide. When the earlier explorers learned of the incident, they set out to stop the Frenchmen, but it was too late, as they had returned to their ship and set sail.

As the ship of captives sailed across the ocean, one by one the little people mysteriously died. Their bodies were tossed overboard. Then some of the French sailors began to die from unknown circumstances as well. By the time the ship reached Europe, none of the little people were left, and less than half of the regular crewmen had survived.

Although the remaining crew members told of the little people, few believed them, and there were no bodies for proof.

Thereafter, the little people around Brockville were very leery of any "big" people. The few that remained moved deeper into the interior and tried to avoid any contact with the outside world.

Since then, and even to this day, sighting one of the wee people occasionally happens, but none of them have been caught. In fact, the wee people are considered quite mysterious and seem to disappear into thin air when

 encountered. This has led to the supposition that the sightings aren't actually living little people, but are the ghosts of those captured by the French many years ago.

In any event, it is considered good luck to catch even a glimpse of a wee person, and extremely bad luck if you attempt to harm them. Any attempt to capture one of them will bring bad fortune on you and your family, so it is best to simply leave them alone.

BETSY'S NIGHTLIGHT

Cape Vincent has a definite French connection. Joseph Bonaparte, Napoleon's brother, resided there in the early 1800s, supposedly paving the way for his brother. Unfortunately, Napoleon never got to enjoy the local scenery, due to untimely imprisonment elsewhere.

Taking pride in the past, there are still French celebrations held every year in the community. Since Horne's Ferry is the only auto ferry crossing the St. Lawrence River to Canada, a multitude of visitors pass through the community annually, and the locals have more than French festivities to offer them.

The city has preserved its history with a museum set in a stone building that once was barracks for soldiers during the War of 1812. There are craft shows, vintage auto shows, and of course a variety of water sports

available to the tourists year around. For those with a hankering for more ghostly entertainment, that is offered as well.

Between Cape Vincent and Millens Bay, along Highway 12E, is a spot that many of the locals claim is haunted. Within sight of the road, but usually unnoticed, is a tiny grave, with a stone wall about two feet high surrounding it. A small tombstone marks the grave, but time and weather have all but obscured the information engraved on it. The old-timers in the area refer to it as Betsy's Grave.

According to stories handed down for generations, the spot is the final resting place of the heroic young daughter of an English missionary back during the 1700s. The missionary lived on one of the islands along with his wife and four-year old daughter, Betsy. There was a cholera epidemic that swept through the area, causing the deaths of many of the residents. Both of Betsy's parents came down with the illness, and were completely disabled. The young girl tended to them to the best of her ability, then realized that she needed help.

Facing a raging blizzard, the young girl set out for the nearest neighbor, who lived a couple miles away. Unfortunately the child succumbed to the storm, and her frozen body was discovered the following day, huddled against an embankment.

The people finding the body recognized the child, and immediately trudged to her home. There they found the afflicted parents, barely alive, but thanks to Betsy's endeavor, both of her folks were attended to and eventually recovered.

The girl was buried at the spot where her body was discovered, and a stone fence was erected around the grave. Her parents diligently visited the grave, frequently after dark. For hours they would sit by the grave with a lantern, as Betsy never liked the dark. By the light of that lantern they would pray and visit with Betsy.

Years later, after both of Betsy's parents had passed away, folks still would occasionally see a light by the grave. If anyone approached the grave to investigate the source of the light, it would either disappear or drift a short distance away. When the investigator moved back, the light would return to the grave. It appeared that someone, or something, was continuing to visit Betsy's grave.

The light is still occasionally seen late at night by people traveling along the road; a faint glow of a lantern held lovingly alongside the gravesite, because Betsy is afraid of the dark.

FEEDING THE GHOSTS

The city of Ogdensburg is located where the Oswegatchie River flows into the St. Lawrence River, near the eastern end of the Thousand Islands Region. With approximately 13,000 residents, it still has small town friendliness, but has cultural opportunities more common to a larger urban city.

The city has many recreational opportunities available,  too. Hiking, swimming, boating, and fishing are popular activities for locals as well as visitors. And as is true with most places with abundant fishing, restaurants are quite plentiful throughout the city.

Serving for many years as the hunting grounds of various tribes of Indians, Ogdensburg was one of the earliest white settlements in that part of the country.

Naturally, where there have been Indians, there are legends that have been handed down over the generations. A legend combining Indian lore and restaurants is alive and well in Ogdensburg.

There is one particular characteristic of many of the restaurants in Ogdensburg where workers are accustomed to their customers leaving a small portion of food on their plates. It has nothing to do with making a statement concerning the quality of the food, and nothing to do with the appetites of the customers. It has to do with old Indian folklore and the large number of descendants from Indians in that area.

According to ancient Indian beliefs, if a person dies honorably, they may be allowed to remain around their family and friends for a while before moving on to the Happy Hunting Grounds. Also, the belief is that the earlier deceased may occasionally be allowed to return and visit their families, not in actual form, but in spiritual form.

In either case, it is believed that the ghosts of these people are nearby, and should be shown the proper attention. To honor and respect these spiritual visitors it is considered important to leave a small portion of food on one's plate for them. Even though the food may not physically disappear, it is thought that by merely being made available to them, it provides nourishment to these ghostly visitors.

Another companion belief is that eating every morsel on one's plate is a sign of disrespect, gluttony, and greed. Leaving a small portion of food is a means of paying respectful homage to the Spirits who helped provide that food. To not do so is to take a chance on angering the Gods and possibly bring famine and other bad luck to the area.

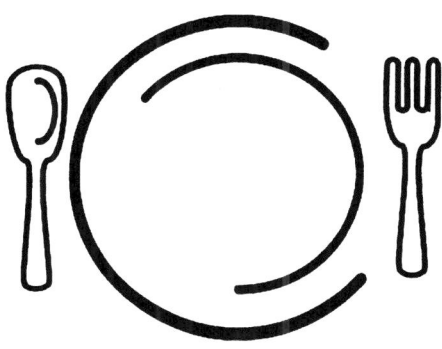

Therefore, no matter how tasty a fillet or other entrée might be, the believers will leave that last bite on the plate for the Spirits.

THE LIGHTS AT TALLEY'S GRAVE

Located on the St. Lawrence River between Brockville and Gananoque, Ontario, is the quaint community of Malloryville. One claim to fame is that it is home to a preserved British gunboat from the War of 1812. The boat was salvaged from the St. Lawrence River near Mallorytown Landing. Another claim to fame is that it was the site of mysterious lights that seemed to haunt the area, witnessed by several generations of the local residents.

A couple miles off the road leading out of Malloryville was the location of a big cherry tree where the mysterious lights and apparitions were reported for many years. Of course there is a legend associated with that tree which tries to explain the ghostly appearances.

Many years ago there was a giant of a man, named Talley, who lived in Malloryville. He was a bachelor with many girlfriends by one account, and a repetitive widower by another. One story claimed that he had been married several times, and each of his wives died under strange circumstances, and he always remarried almost immediately. Since the two stories have similar themes, we'll follow the widower version.

As grumpy and withdrawn as Talley was, people were always surprised at how quickly he found someone who'd marry him. Some supposed it was for the money he might have, and others were less kind in their gossiping.

Nevertheless, his last marriage only lasted a few months, and then his wife disappeared. He claimed that she ran off somewhere, but nobody knew for certain.

Anyway, he never remarried after that one, and lived alone in a small cabin for the duration of his life.

As he advanced in age, old man Talley liked to go into town and sit around one of the stores, listening to some of the men spin yarns. Talley would seldom offer any stories of his own; in fact, he seldom said anything at all. He'd just sit in a chair, listening, and eating cherries from a paper sack.

One fateful day Talley popped a large cherry in his mouth and, although nobody noticed until it was too late, the cherry pit hung in his throat and choked him. The first anyone noticed was when old Talley fell out of his chair onto the floor. By then he'd already stopped breathing, and was dead as a doornail.

Back then, family cemeteries were common, so Talley was laid to rest on the back corner of his property. According to some 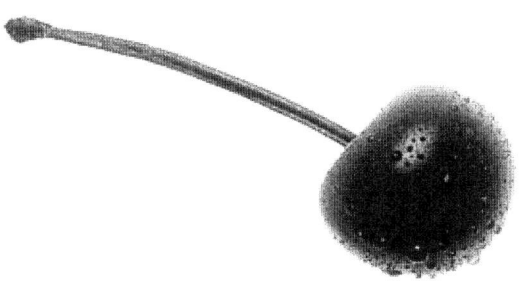 stories, a couple of his wives had been buried there, too, but Talley was too cheap to put any kind of marker on their graves.

Nobody paid much attention for a few years, but then it was discovered that a cherry tree had grown on Talley's grave, just about where his big old head would have been. Again, nobody thought much about it, and left well enough alone.

Then people began seeing lights out around that cherry tree. Sometimes it would be a single light, and sometimes it would be two, three, or more. The lights would dance all up and down the branches of that cherry tree. The actual source of the lights was a mystery.

Some people claimed to have seen a large dark form, shaped like a big man, standing by the tree trunk, with the lights moving all up and down him. If the observer drew closer, the figure would seem to melt right into the trunk of the tree, and the lights would fade completely away.

This phenomenon of mystifying lights was frequently seen by the people around Malloryville for many years. They were called, "Talley's Wives" by some of the locals, and it was claimed that the balls of light were the ghosts of Talley's wives, come back to haunt his grave.

Another strange thing was, although the tree was full of blooms each spring, it never bore the first cherry. During a thunderstorm one turbulent night, lightning struck the cherry tree, splitting it nearly in two. After that people claimed to occasionally hear a loud groaning sound emitting from the tree, as if it was in agony.

Still, the mystery lights continued to be seen regularly. The unexplained sightings didn't stop until the tree was totally rotten and had fallen over. Then the lights or apparition were never seen again.

THE OUTLAW GOLD

One of the favorite places along the St. Lawrence River for history buffs to visit is the town of Prescott. It is home to the Fort Wellington National Historic Site of Canada, where there are well preserved buildings dating back to the 1830s. An authentically costumed staff demonstrates the everyday life of a soldier and his family during that period.

Prescott also houses the Forwarders' Museum in the downtown area, and, lastly, the Battle of the Windmill National Historic Site of Canada. Many festivities adorn the scenic waterfront, leaving the impression of an idyllic little community. It wasn't always that friendly and innocent, according to a century-old story of intrigue.

Back in the late 1800s an interesting story began making the rounds near Prescott. According to rumors, outlaws from the United States escaped into Canada after robbing a train of a large gold shipment. The money was being sent to a major bank in New York, but the train was waylaid by the robbers. There was a gang of five men, and they rode into Prescott with large saddlebags on each of their horses.

The men hung around town for several days, but seemed to spend quite a bit of time somewhere west of town. Then there was a big argument during a poker game one night, and gunfire erupted. When the smoke cleared, three townspeople and four of the outlaws were dead. The fifth outlaw was arrested and promptly hanged.

There was an old drunk who shared a cell with the outlaw prior to the hanging, and he claimed that the doomed man confessed that he had helped bury a fortune in gold west of Prescott. The drunk claimed to have some particular knowledge that could lead to the discovery of the gold.

Naturally there were those who believed the drunk, and others who claimed it was simply drunken ravings for attention. Regardless of the veracity of the story, the drunk enlisted a couple of believers to go treasure hunting with him, promising them an even split of the loot.

A couple of days later one of the believers staggered into town, barely alive. Questioned, he reported that the others had been killed by something too terrible to describe. Then he, too, died, although there were no visible injuries to his body.

Since then, many people have gone in search for the outlaws' gold, but nobody has ever claimed to have been successful in finding it. Instead, the people who thought they were close to the treasure always were chased away by strange happenings.

Some claim to have seen ghostly apparitions of the outlaws, still guarding the treasure. Others say that unexplained things happened, such as suddenly getting strong feelings of dread or uneasiness. Some claim that they suffered partial paralysis, and one claimed that he suddenly woke up miles from where he was supposed to be, with no earthly idea of how he got there. One man claimed to have seen a face of pure evil staring at him from the trunk of a tree. That was enough for him to give up the search.

Even today occasionally a map will turn up, reportedly leading to the gold, but interest in pursuing the treasure has dwindled. The fear of the supernatural seems to be stronger than the desire for the gold. In any event, the outlaws seem to continue being the unyielding possessors of their stolen loot, protecting it even in death.

THE MISSING BIBLES

With expansive waterfront along the St. Lawrence River, Waddington, New York, provides opportunities for boating, fishing, water-skiing, tubing, or simply watching passing ships along the river. It has sandy beaches, exquisite restaurants, and friendly bed-and-breakfast lodging for its visitors.

The town was originally named Hamilton, after Alexander Hamilton, who was associated with the town's earliest landowners, but later changed to the present Waddington. The town is only minutes away from five colleges and universities in St. Lawrence County, and part of its dubious history is tied to one of the colleges.

The community of Waddington made state-wide news around 1952 when a couple of college students selling

Bibles disappeared after last being seen there. At the time it was common for students to travel around the country during their summer break, selling Bibles door-to-door in order to finance their college education. That summer a young boy and girl arrived in Waddington driving a 1949 Ford sedan loaded with Bibles. They had just finished their second year of school at a small college in upstate New York.

It was typical for these students to stay in a small town for a day or two, and then move on, so nobody thought much about it when the young people apparently left.

Then a week or two later, the local authorities were notified that the couple was missing, and inquiries were made as to where they had last been seen. It seems that none of their relatives or supervisors had any knowledge of the students after they sold a few Bibles in the town of Waddington.

The relatives of the couple, as well as the local police, scoured the area, but came up with no leads as to the whereabouts of the missing students.

The following spring was unusually dry, and the river near Waddington was lower than normal. Some fishermen discovered an automobile submerged near the bank of the river. With the level of the water down, they could make out the top of the car a few feet underwater.

Authorities were called, and the car was pulled from the river. It turned out to be a 1949 Ford sedan, the same vehicle that the students had been driving. The car was

empty; no bodies, no luggage, and no Bibles.

The nearest house to the scene was a two-story home belonging to the LeFleur family. This was a thirty-something-year old childless couple who had built the house three or four years earlier. The couple was questioned, but couldn't recall hearing or seeing anything unusual around the time that the students disappeared, and said that the students had not come to their house with their Bibles.

With no clues, the strange incident soon moved from front page news to an occasional comment in beauty parlor gossip.

About fifteen years later, Mr. LeFleur died of a sudden heart attack. Mrs. LeFleur lived alone for another thirty of so years. What people remembered most about her was that she never showed her age very much, appearing much younger than she actually was. Although friendly enough to those she encountered in town, Mrs. LeFleur lived an almost reclusive life, seldom leaving the house except for necessary shopping, and never having any visitors.

After she died, leaving no will or known relatives, the house was eventually auctioned off. The next owner did not live in the house but a few months, and then sold it. The following owners never stayed for long in the house either. It gradually became known that the residents kept hearing unexplained noises in the house; sounds of moaning and crying. There were also reports that an apparition of a distressed young girl would occasionally be glimpsed in a corner of the kitchen. Sometimes she would be dressed in a dark dress, and other times she would be wearing a solid white dress. The apparition would only appear for a second, and then disappear. Soon the empty house stayed on the market for over a year, but no buyer could be found.

Then one night the house burned to the ground. It was thought that perhaps it had been stuck by lightning, but there was no evidence to support that.

The property was eventually taken over by the city. During the cleanup of the burned rubble, it was discovered that there had been a basement in the house.

None of the recent residents had known it was there. A cleverly hidden trap-door in the corner of the kitchen led down a narrow set of steps into a full basement, apparently dug by hand.

The discovery of the basement was not the main surprise, however. There were chains with manacles attached to the beams along the basement walls. There was a long wooden blood-stained table in the center of the room. A stockade-type chair with well-worn, rotting leather straps on the arms and legs was setting at one end of the table. There were several rusty knives and leather whips strewn across the floor. Five shallow graves were found at one end of the basement containing the remains of five people, two males and three females.

And over in a corner of the basement, covered with an old quilt, were three boxes neatly stacked. The musty boxes were full of Bibles.

THE PIPE-SMOKING GHOST

Alexandria Bay is a resort community located on the St. Lawrence River in the midst of the Thousand Islands. It has extraordinary scenery and is in a position to be the central point for visits throughout the islands. It

 depends heavily on the summer tourist season, and its activity drops considerably during the winter.

In the midst of the bay is Wolfe Island, home to the famous Boldt Castle. Another major tourist attraction, Singer Castle, is a few miles away on Dark Island. While Boldt Castle was built around a love story, Singer Castle is known for intricate architecture, gorgeous furnishings, and puzzling secret passages allowing the owner to spy on his guests.

During the summer months, Alexandria Bay is alive with tourists, and there are many attractions to keep them busy. In additional to water sports, there are museums, craft stores, and superb dining available. There are several popular lodges, some of which provide sufficient amenities as to keep their guests entertained right there on their premises. One such lodge has apparently kept one of its employees on the premises, even after his death. At least that is the story often told there.

This particular lodge near Alexandria Bay has served tourists for decades. It has a party boat that takes the guests out for a tour on the river. For many years the

boat was captained by a man known as Uncle Thurmond. Uncle Thurmond was a retired sea captain who seemed to take great pleasure in ferrying the guests around and telling sea stories.

The lodge has a restaurant with an outdoor deck for dining outside, weather permitting. On any Saturday night with decent weather, Uncle Thurmond would take up residence at a corner table and spin yarn after yarn to an enthralled audience. One interesting thing is that Uncle Thurmond had an exceptional rapport with teenagers. Young people who claimed to be bored with everything else, gathered around him as if drawn by a magnet. Being around the young people seemed to energize Uncle Thurmond, so it was a happy relationship.

Uncle Thurmond almost always smoked a pipe with a sweet cherry fragrance of tobacco. Whenever people saw him lighting up his pipe, they knew that a good story was about to begin.

Unfortunately, one winter Uncle Thurmond came down with pneumonia and died within the week. He had been such a fixture at the lodge for so long that he was sorely missed. There were people who vacationed at the lodge year after year who looked forward to visiting with Uncle Thurmond.

One Saturday night, about a month after his funeral, a worker at the restaurant came in from the deck with an astonishing report. He claimed that he'd gotten a strong whiff of sweet cherry tobacco as he passed by the corner outside table.

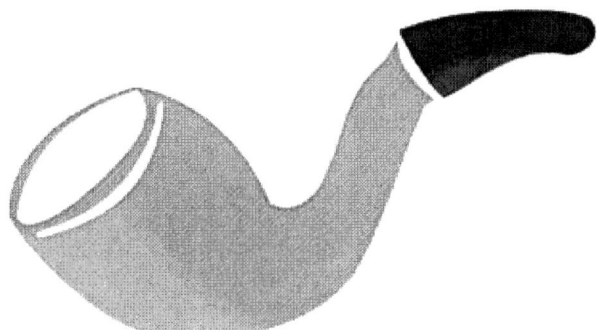

Others began encountering that same thing. It would always be on a Saturday night, and it always seemed to come from the area of that corner table. Investigations turned up no explanation, and it has continued to be reported to this day. Some say that Uncle Thurmond wasn't quite ready to leave the lodge and his friends. His spirit continues to hang around the lodge and its people.

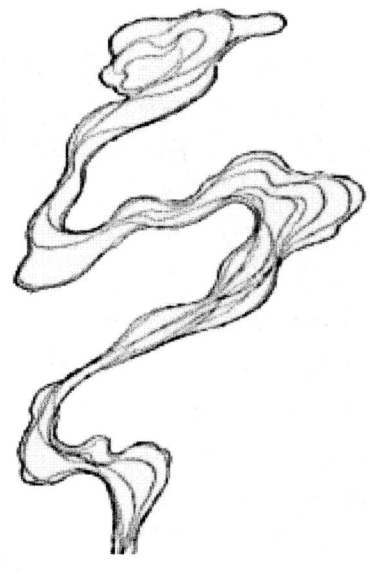

THE RIVER GHOST

As far back as the late 1800s, people have claimed to see a mermaid along the banks of the river near Morrisburg, Ontario. Others say it is just the ghost of a young girl named Sarah.

Sarah came from a wealthy family, and her folks became quite distressed when she fell head over heels in love with a dashing young fisherman known as J.T. to everyone.

J.T. was quite the womanizer, and could be seen with a different lady about every week. Nevertheless, Sarah thought that she could tame him, and paid no heed to the warnings of her parents. Although J.T. did seem to settle on Sarah for about a month, rumors abounded that he was seeing a couple of other girls at nearby Massena, just across the St. Lawrence River.

Sarah's father was quite irate, and hired a couple of toughs to rough up J.T., hoping to teach him a lesson. The roughing up session got totally out of hand, and J.T. ended up dead.

Sarah, of course, was heartbroken and could not be consoled. She felt that she'd lost her one true love, and totally discounted any tales of him being unfaithful. Plus, she blamed her father for J.T.'s death, and she actually had a pretty good argument there.

So distraught was the young lady that about a week after his death, she was found floating in the river near her home. Her death was ruled a tragic suicide.

Shortly afterwards, and continuing to this day, people began seeing a dark figure of a young girl along the river. Sometimes she would be floating in the river or lying half in and half out of the water. This gave rise to the mermaid version.

Other times she would be standing or walking along the riverbank, gazing forlornly out across the water as if searching for her lover. She has also been seen strolling across the water, her ghostly body refusing to sink into the depths that once claimed her life.

She is known by the local people as, "Sarah, the River Ghost."

THE DEVIL'S CREW

One of the many mysteries surrounding the St. Lawrence Seaway involves the boat simply referred to as the Devil's Crew.

In the 1880s there was quite a lot of shipping traffic around Sackets Harbor. Late one afternoon this ship came slowly floating into the harbor. It pulled up to a

dock in an expert manner and stopped. Dockhands quickly secured the ship with ropes, but noticed that there was not any of the crew visible. Usually there would be several crewmen assisting with the docking.

When they boarded the ship, they were astonished to find that every solitary crewman on the ship was dead. Since there was not a mark on any of the bodies, it was as if they had all dropped dead at their posts.

Nobody could explain the mass deaths, nor could they explain how the ship managed to expertly dock itself.

In the early 1900s a number of people on that same dock witnessed an old sailing ship approaching them. When it drew closer, the people reported seeing a skeleton crew, literally, sailing the ship. Skeletons could be seen scampering around on the deck of the ship, as if preparing to dock.

Instead of coming to a halt at the dock, however, the ghost ship slowly disappeared as it passed into the dock area. It seemed quite real one moment, and the next moment it had vanished.

It was discovered that the day was the anniversary of the arrival of the ship with the dead crew. Some thirty years later, again on the anniversary date, more than a dozen people witnessed that same skeleton-crewed ship arrive in the exact same manner. The apparition became known as the Devil's Crew, and it still occasionally makes its ghostly docking in Sackets Harbor.

THE GHOSTS OF THE TWO BROTHERS

Aided by its close proximity to several popular islands in the Thousand Islands chain, Gananoque is one of the favorite fishing communities along the St. Lawrence

River. Once the Thousand Islands Region was discovered to be a great summer haven, people from the United States, as well as Canada, saw the benefits to the area being a vacation destination. As early as the 1870s guest cottages began popping up along the nearby islands, and the Gananoque community became one of the more important Canadian riverfront towns.

With its growing popularity, a resort inn was built in 1896, occupying land originally housing the Gananoque Carriage Works. The picturesque location made a natural setting for a summer hotel for the increasing number of tourists to the region.

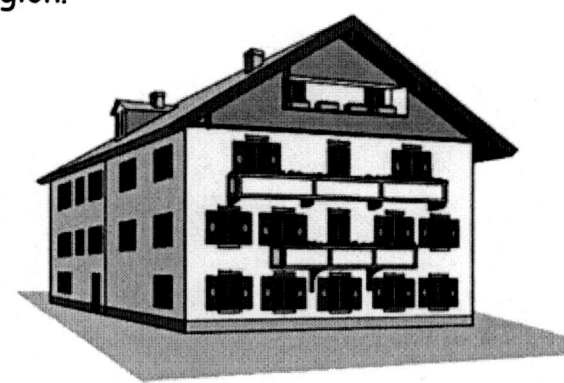

A large portion of the inn was destroyed by fire in 1907, but was quickly rebuilt. Though it has changed hands many times over the ensuing decades, and has been renovated countless times, Gananoque Inn is still an important historic icon of the area.

Even though the community is known for its hospitality and friendly people, it also has a dark shadow in its past. There is a skeleton in its closet that is still talked about today.

During the late 1800s two brothers built a large house on the outskirts of Gananoque. They had suddenly come into a fortune, and they were intent on living lavishly. It wasn't clear where their newfound wealth originated; some said they'd found gold, while others thought they had gotten rich through illicit smuggling activities. Nevertheless, they were wealthy and made no secret of it.

They were known to throw extravagant parties at their mansion that would sometimes last for several days.

Drinking, dancing, and gambling were frequently occurring day and night at the place. There were whispers among the local gossips of much more debauchery.

One day, after one of the multi-day parties, the brothers got into an argument and fought a duel. One of them was killed instantly, and the other one died the following day from his wounds.

The house passed into the hands of a wealthy banker. He lived in the house less than a month before his wife was killed. The banker was supposedly cleaning a pistol in their bedroom, the gun went off accidentally, and the wife was shot in the head.

There were rumors that it was not an accident, but that the banker had accused her of an indiscretion which she adamantly denied. There was a quick investigation, but no charges were filed. The banker, seemingly distraught, sold the house and moved from the area.

The next owner of the house was an elderly couple. They only lived there a week when one of their grandchildren drowned in the nearby river. They moved from the house the next day.

The house stayed vacant for nearly a year, and then burned to the ground one night. The cause of the fire was not determined, but arson was suspected.

The property was purchased and a hotel was planned for the location. During the construction, one worker fell from a scaffold and broke his neck, and then another worker was maimed when the blade of a bench saw came loose. Before the building was completed, it, too, burned mysteriously.

Now the location is a park, with trees, trails, and a fountain. The peaceful scene can be deceiving, however. Seldom has a year gone by without someone reporting a mysterious sighting of lights moving around the area late at night. The lights appear to travel slowly, but either fade out or dart quickly away if approached.

Shadowy figures are frequently seen beside the trails by those brave enough to venture along them at night. The figures appear to be fighting, and sounds of arguing have been heard. Again, if approached, the figures disappear into thin air.

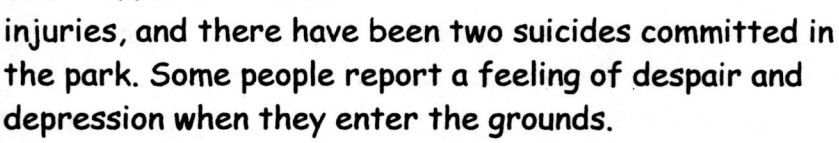

There have been numerous accidents in the park, too. Bike riders have found themselves flung over their handlebars, skateboarders have suffered serious injuries, and there have been two suicides committed in the park. Some people report a feeling of despair and depression when they enter the grounds.

Many of the local people avoid visiting the park altogether as it is rumored to be cursed. The feuding brothers of the original mansion are thought to be haunting the park, just as they did the other residents of the property. They were deceitful in life, and are treacherous in death.

THE GHOST OF LOVE LOST

Cornwall is known as the "Friendly Seaway City." It is one of the older cities along the seaway, and is proud of its rich history. It has several museums, open air concerts during the summer months, and a replica of an 1800s working farm. It even has the Lost Villages

Museum, a tribute to the six villages lost to flooding as a direct result of the St. Lawrence Seaway during the 1950s.

There is a multitude of attractions for the outdoor enthusiasts, too. Cycle paths, hiking trails, and many water sports are available for the visitors. Its waterfront beaches, parks, and camping areas are also known for a more sinister reason. This involves the tragic love story of one of Cornwall's early inhabitants.

There was a beautiful young girl in Cornwall who was courted by two young men of the town. She would be seen with first one of the men, then the other, letting neither know which one was her favorite.

One of the men came from a wealthy family, and the other one was the son of a poor fisherman. While one was constantly lavishing expensive gifts on the lady, the other one had nothing to offer but his company.

Naturally the two rivals grew jealous of each other, with both trying to get the lady to commit to them.

Eventually there was a mix-up over which of the suitors was accompanying the lady to a party, and their disagreement moved to the edge of the river bank. During the ensuing fight, the two combatants fell into the river, still battling in a fierce struggle. Unfortunately, the man from the wealthy family was drowned during the scuffle.

The suitor from the poor family knew that he would have no chance at a trial, and would likely be hanged or sent to prison for life. Frightened, he took flight, soon managing to sign on as a crew member of a ship sailing to Europe. Ships were almost always looking for crew members, and generally asked no questions.

The young lady was distraught, as she suddenly had gone from two adamant suitors to none. She was frequently seen by the river bank staring at the ruthless water that had taken both of her loves from her.

After several months, the lady decided that the sailor was not going to return, and married the younger brother of the wealthy suitor. Though she was given a mansion

and any earthly possession her heart desired, she still frequently walked the river bank late in the evenings. During a cold spell, she caught pneumonia and died.

Even in death she still mourns her first loves, as her ghost refuses to rest in peace. Seldom does a month pass that someone doesn't see the figure of a lady dressed in black, standing on the river bank, staring despondently into the unforgiving water.

THE DRAFT-DODGER GHOST

During the Vietnam War there were quite a number of young men from the United States seeking refuge in Canada. Known by the term "draft-dodgers," these youngsters knew that they were about to be called into military service, and were willing to leave their home country in order to avoid it.

One such young man arrived alone in Kingston. He obtained lodging at a nice apartment, and began to be seen around town. Seeming to be well-funded, he frequented the local night spots, spending money freely and not doing any type of work. He became part of the local drug culture, and was stoned virtually every night.

This lifestyle lasted for several months, and then his funds apparently dried up. He was still seen at the night spots, but had less and less money to spend. Many of the friends he'd made when he had money drifted quickly away from him. After failing to pay rent for a couple of months, he was evicted from his apartment. Broke and destitute, he scavenged along the streets briefly, and then was found hanging from a tree near the apartment building where he had lived.

There were rumors that he'd gotten deeply in debt with a drug dealer and had a price on his head, but his death was ruled a suicide. Most of the local people thought

"good riddance" and went on with their lives.

The young man's spirit was not ready, or could not, leave the area however. People began reporting seeing a body hanging from the tree where he had died. Upon closer inspection, nothing was ever found, but a week or two later someone else would report the same sight.

Someone cut the tree down one night, but the ghostly spirit still haunts the site. People still report seeing a dark figure of a man, swaying back and forth as if hanging from a tree no longer there.

THE THEATRE GHOST OF KINGSTON

One of the favorite haunts of ghosts is a theatre. Not the type that shows movies, but the ones that have had live stage performances. There is something about that setting that makes a perfect environment for ghosts.

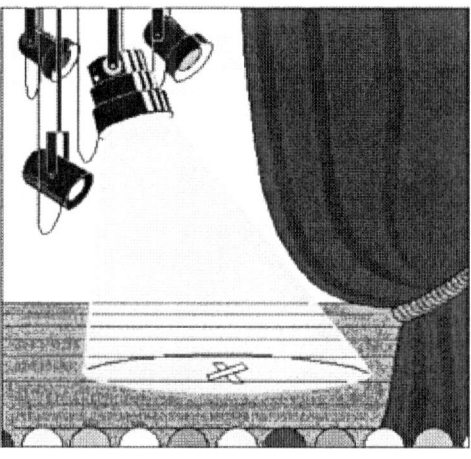

For many years there was just such a theatre in Kingston. The building began as a movie theatre, but that closed during the 1950s. The building was vacant for seven or eight years, and then reopened as a community theatre. A few of the front rows of seats were removed in order to erect a stage and a backstage area.

Not long after the first play was produced, strange things began to occur, and ghosts were suspected. Some claimed that the ghosts originated due to a rumored killing in the theatre while it was vacant. Most people, however, attribute it to the ghostly attraction to theatres.

The first reported incidents involved props being mysteriously moved about. Some items would vanish for a day or so, and then turn up, either exactly where they should have been, or at some totally inappropriate place.

Lights in the theatre would suddenly dim, or go completely out for a few seconds, then come back to their original brightness. Although the electrical wiring was thoroughly checked, no problems could be detected.

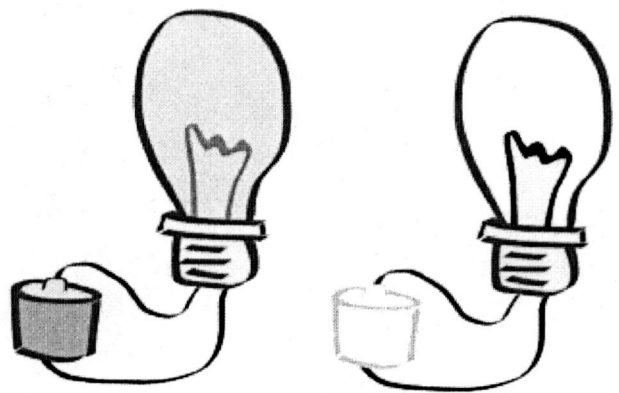

During late night rehearsals, sounds would frequently be heard from an area of the theatre that was unoccupied. People claimed to sometimes hear the faint sound of a violin, but the source could not be traced.

Then, late at night, the figure of a small man began to be seen. In the most common sightings the man would be seen near the back of the auditorium. Occasionally he would be glimpsed in the hallway leading to the dressing rooms. Each time the man would simply disappear into the floor or wall.

Once, though nobody saw him at the time it was made, a cast photograph seemed to include the figure. Along with a dozen smiling actors lined up at the front of the stage, a shadowy silhouette stood behind them by the curtain. It appeared to be a small man observing the photography session.

Since the ghostly apparition seemed to have no malice, other than occasionally messing with the props, he became an accepted part of the theatre. For some reason, he was given the name, "Falstaff."

There was never an agreement on why Falstaff decided to dwell in that theatre, but he was seen at least three or four times a year until the theatre was torn down. Perhaps that allowed him to find peace, or at least move along to someplace else to haunt.

THE GHOSTS OF BOLDT CASTLE

George Boldt was a wealthy hotel owner from New York City. He was a self-made millionaire, known for his acute business sense. He left quite a legacy, as we shall see.

One of several things credited to George Boldt is the naming of the salad topping named after the islands, Thousand Island Dressing. Even this event seems somewhat shrouded in mystery.

One version of the origin of the famous dressing involves Sophie LaLonde, of Clayton, New York. She served the dressing at a dinner for her guests; it was well received; and she later gave the recipe for the topping to Clayton hotel owner Ella Bertrand and New York City stage actress May Irwin. Ms. Irwin in turn shared it with the hotel magnate George

Boldt, and he took it and ran, giving the dressing its name.

There is, however, a slightly different version of the salad dressing's origin. George Boldt and his wife Louise fell in love with the Thousand Islands Region's exquisite beauty during the 1890s. They frequently brought their friends along for a cruise aboard their yacht in the Thousand Islands. During one of these cruises in 1894, the Boldts' personal chef created a special salad dressing for their dinner. The guests were so complimentary of the topping that George Boldt quickly saw an opportunity. He introduced the dressing at the Waldorf Astoria Hotel in New York City, and called it "Thousand Islands Dressing" in honor of the region where it was first prepared.

The two versions agree that Boldt took advantage of a good thing when he tasted it, and the dressing went on to increase his wealth considerably.

Another lasting monument to the Boldt name is Boldt Castle, located on Heart Island in Alexandria Bay. The legend behind the castle is a sad love story. George Boldt commissioned the design and construction of the castle on the heart-shaped island in honor of his beloved wife Louise.

The plans called for an elaborate design of six stories with 120 rooms, along the lines of a Rhineland Castle style. There would be a drawbridge, beautiful gardens, a children's playhouse, tunnels, a powerhouse, and an ornate stone archway at the shoreline of the island, welcoming the arriving people. Soon work was well under way on the eleven buildings comprising the compound, with hopes of it being completed so that George could present it to his wife on Valentine's Day.

Unfortunately, Louise died suddenly in January 1904, and George immediately halted the construction. It stood in a state of incompletion, exposed to the forces of nature until 1977. Then the Thousand Islands Bridge Authority undertook the task of refurbishing and restoring the castle to the point of when the original construction was discontinued. The castle was eventually opened as a tourist attraction, and has proven to be quite popular to this day.

With such a heart-wrenching history, of course the castle has its share of legends associated with it. For many years people on tour boats approaching the island have reported seeing the figure of a woman walking slowly along the shoreline. She is always wearing a long black dress and has a black veil concealing her face. She seems to be watching the approaching boat, but as it draws closer, her body slowly fades away. This figure is thought to be the ghost of Louise, mourning the failure of ever getting to live in the castle being built for her.

Another apparition frequently observed over the years is generally referred to as "Ghost George." 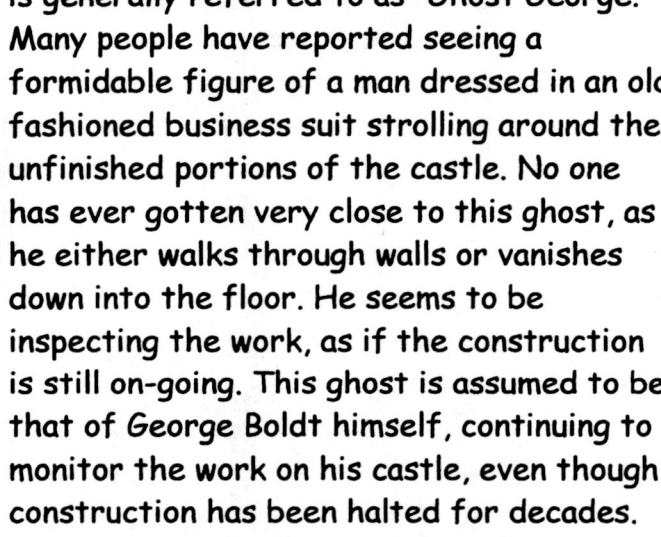 Many people have reported seeing a formidable figure of a man dressed in an old fashioned business suit strolling around the unfinished portions of the castle. No one has ever gotten very close to this ghost, as he either walks through walls or vanishes down into the floor. He seems to be inspecting the work, as if the construction is still on-going. This ghost is assumed to be that of George Boldt himself, continuing to monitor the work on his castle, even though construction has been halted for decades.

There have also been reports of people hearing footsteps in the hallways, but no person visible to have caused the sounds. Others have heard whispered voices behind closed doors, but upon opening the doors, the rooms are vacant.

If these are ghosts, they seem to be harmless, and are simply welcomed. After all, what self-respecting castle would not have at least one resident ghost?

THE RUM-RUNNER GHOSTS

The Eighteenth Amendment to the Constitution of the United States began the Prohibition Era. Since the manufacture and sale of liquor was prohibited, naturally a number of enterprising souls saw an opportunity to exploit the people's thirst. The Thousand Islands Region was an ideal location, providing countless hiding places amidst the many islands with secluded coves, as well as easy access to border-crossing. Soon the area was literally flooded with what was known as "rum-runners."

One story was that a wealthy American bought one of the islands and constructed a giant vault in which to stock liquor from Canada. With speedy boats and knowledgeable boatmen, the liquor could be easily transported across the river under cover of darkness.

Supposedly a cabin on one of the islands was set up as a gambling parlor by this same American. United States officials were frequently invited to card parties at the cabin, and always seemed to be quite lucky. The rumor was that as the hired card players purposefully kept the officials' attention by playing their cards carelessly and letting the officials win, the rum-running boats were

busily speeding back and forth across the river with their illegal cargo.

There were many drinking establishments set up on the Canadian islands where the Americans eagerly journeyed for their liquor. Drinking, gambling, and prostitution were only a short boat ride away. Liquor and money flowed freely throughout the region.

All good things come to an end, and a lot of people became unemployed when Prohibition was repealed. There remain reminders of that era around and beneath the islands. The liquor was frequently transported by the rum-runners in gunny sacks. If the boats were in danger of being caught, the sacks would be tossed overboard, thus leaving no evidence. To this day divers sometimes run across liquor bottles during forays beneath the river, particularly close to the United States shoreline.

An entirely different reminder is also regularly reported by the people living and visiting the island area. For the past 50 years there have been reports of phantom boats zipping in and out between some of the islands. According to descriptions, the people see a dark outline of a boat speeding across the river. Sometimes there is no sound associated with it, and sometimes there will be the sound of a revving motor, but not a boat in sight.

Some people claim that they have seen men in the boats, and there have been eye-witness reports that the figures are skeletons. Usually the witnesses are not close enough to the boats to distinguish anything other than the outline of these ghostly rum-runners who apparently refuse to stop their nightly excursions with the illegal cargo.

THE GHOSTS OF THE $1000 CASINO

A large casino was constructed on one of the islands near Alexandria Bay shortly after the Prohibition Era began. It was owned and controlled by one of the mob syndicates from New York City. In honor of the name of the islands, as well as to attract wealthy gamblers, the

place was named The $1000 Casino.

People from both countries flocked to the casino, as tourist boats were provided for easy access from both shores. These boats made several trips each night bringing the people and their money to the island.

It was an impressive building with elaborate grounds, and an expanse of lights that could be seen for miles. A large water fountain greeted the visitors, and it was considered lucky to toss a few coins in the fountain to help determine one's success inside.

The main casino was on the first floor of the building, with an impressive array of gambling machines and tables available for those eager to part with their money. Well dressed staff members were ready to politely assist with the separation of that money.

On the second floor was a restaurant with an expansive menu, certain to please the most discriminating diners. An open air balcony afforded outside dining with an exquisite view of the casino grounds, the river, and lights on the far shore.

There were discreet stairways leading to the third floor of the building. It was rumored to have a number of small, sound-proofed rooms, and a bevy of beautiful women fit to populate a king's harem.

On the main floor were a couple of separate rooms set aside for particularly high-rollers, with tightly controlled access. These gamblers did not have to rub elbows with the common people. Free food, drinks, and pretty hostesses were provided to keep the clients happy as they lost large sums of their money to the casino.

Of course an enterprise of this nature required tight security. Not only were guards necessary to watch over the large amount of money on the grounds, the identities of some of the clients were just as judiciously protected. There were private entrances available to the privileged clients who did not wish to be seen in the main casino. A special boat could whisk a person to the island, he could enter through a private entrance, and later leave the same way, with little chance of anyone even knowing that he was ever there.

Also inherent to an establishment of this type, there were occasionally "problems." Sometimes a losing gambler might get a little loud and rowdy. These types were

 usually hustled outside by a bouncer and given a chance to cool down. There were also the people who got in over their head with their losses. These people were not tolerated, as it was bad for business to allow such things to go unheeded.

This leads to the rumor of there being a special "cooling down" building at the back of the casino, down close to a particular dock. Clients deemed to be out of control, and perhaps those who foolishly threatened reprisals, were dealt with swiftly. Legend has it that many people were dispatched right in that building. Others, and perhaps the bodies of the first types, were given a one-way boat ride out into the bay. Stories insist that many poor gamblers wound up at the bottom of the river weighted down with "concrete boots."

The casino became involved in a quarrel between two mob "families" after a couple of years. Prosperity breeds greed, and in this case, an attempted takeover. After several major skirmishes, the casino mysteriously burned to the ground, and after one attempt to rebuild it failed, the grounds were abandoned.

That's not the end of the story, however. A private mansion was later constructed on the island near the original site of the casino. An elaborate summer home, it has changed hands frequently through the years, with nobody living in it more than a couple of summers.

For financial reasons, the house has never openly been admitted to be haunted, but rumors abound of several strange occurrences there. Frequent sightings of apparitions running frantically along the shoreline have been reported. Several claims of residents seeing the figure of a hanged man dangling from a tree limb behind the mansion have leaked to the public.

Screams of terror have been heard late at night, coming from the edge of the island, but no source for the screams could ever be found. The most morbid phenomenon reported, however, was rumored to be the final straw for several of the residents. They described seeing one or more bodies of bloated, drowned men floating up to the boat dock. These men would typically stare up at the residents with unseeing eyes, and then sink slowly beneath the water. Divers and rescue crews

called to the scene have never found any such thing beneath the surface.

People familiar with the island's sordid history attribute the reports to the spirits of the casino's victims, still haunting the place where they were murdered. Of course there are a number of people who are not aware of the island's past. Those are the source for the mansion's next buyer.

THE MYSTIQUE OF SINGER CASTLE

One of the larger islands in the chain is called Dark Island. It got its name from the early seamen. To the people approaching the island from the river, as well as from nearby Ingleneuk Island, it always appeared very dark due to its high granite peak heavily covered with giant pine trees.

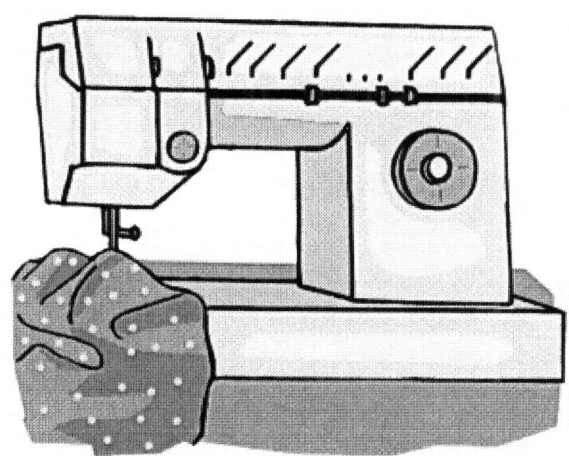

In the early 1900s the island was purchased by Frederick Bourne, of Singer Sewing Machine fame. With the intention of having a hunting lodge built on the island, he commissioned the construction. The architect designed it along the lines of an English castle, complete with a four story clock tower with six-foot diameter clock faces. (These faces were rumored to be of pure gold. The clock still chimes every fifteen minutes, ironically marking the passage of time on this otherwise timeless island.)

Tons of granite were quarried from nearby Oak Island for the construction of the lodge. Many loads of soil were hauled to the island to cover the rocky surface. Although it was originally known as "The Towers," it later was changed to simply "Singer Castle."

Bourne had worked his way up the ladder and became head of the Singer Company at the young age of thirty-six. He and his wife Emma had nine children. He was considered a keen businessman and very charitable to his community. True to the name of the island, however, Bourne apparently had a dark side, too.

The castle has many halls, rooms with antique furnishings, a squash court, and a magnificent view of the St. Lawrence River. It also has a dungeon, many secret passageways, and tunnels connecting the various buildings on the island. Many of the walls are adorned with what could be called "suggestive" paintings. The exact intent of these little extras remains shrouded in mystery.

At the front of the castle is a massive medieval entranceway to greet the visitors. Inside is an enormous marble fireplace, and then a marble stairway leads to the

Breakfast Room. From there is an extraordinary view of the river below.

But then there is the beautiful walnut-paneled library that has a secret panel connecting to passages within the castle walls. A portrait conceals a spy hole from one of the secret passageways. There are many grates built into walls allowing spying from places of concealment in the  secret passageways. A person knowledgeable of the castle's secrets could spy on guests from a variety of places, and could easily move undetected throughout the structure along the passageways behind the walls.

The purpose or use of the castle's secrets is not known. The existence of the passageways and spy holes became widely revealed only after the possession of the castle passed from the Bourne family in the middle 1960s.

The castle is a very popular tourist attraction today. Tour boats bring guests to the island, and tour guides take them on a forty-five minute narrative tour of the grounds and buildings. In fact, the entire island can be rented for weddings, parties, etc. However, this isn't a place for the squeamish.

Many people report having a strange feeling come over them as soon as they enter the castle. These feelings are increased dramatically in certain of the rooms. The library is one room that frequently gives visitors a creepy feeling. People describe having a sensation of being watched. This occurs not only in the library, but in many other locations throughout the castle. Perhaps they are.

Even the staff has heard the sounds of footsteps behind the walls. This has occurred when they were positive that nobody could be in the secret passageways. They attribute it to a ghost of the Bourne family, still spying on guests.

There are pictures on the walls that refuse to stay straight. There was one picture that refused to stay hung. Time after time a staff member would find it propped on the floor below where it was supposed to hang. Eventually this picture was placed in storage, as no one could explain its movements.

The castle may still have more secrets to be discovered. There has long been a rumor of vicious happenings concerning the dungeon in the 1920s or 1930s, and the existence of tortured spirits remaining there. Occasional moaning sounds  from that area have been heard, but not explained, for decades.

There are also rumors that the castle has secret panels and possibly small rooms that have yet to be discovered. Some think that Frederick Bourne's ghost still resides in one of these secret rooms, and that it is he who roams the passageways late at night. Are these rumors merely gossip? Spend a night at the castle and find out for yourself!

THE MILLIONAIRE'S GHOST

  When the Thousand Islands Region was recognized as a prestigious summer home haven, it suddenly became popular among wealthy families to purchase their own individual island. A number of businessmen from New York City and Philadelphia began buying small islands on the American side of the St. Lawrence River.

  Instead of small vacation cabins cropping up, however, these people began having mansions built on their property.

Each new construction seemed bent on out-doing anything previously constructed. Not only did these mansions have expansive square footage, elaborate furnishings, and ornate decorations inside the house, but gardeners were imported from as far away as Italy to construct magnificent gardens outside.

Each of these homes was worthy of a king, and cost a king's ransom to build. This stretch of islands with these splendid mansions became known as Millionaire's Row.

The people with homes along this stretch included many of the more famous families of the United States. All through the summer season there would be elaborate parties, with the families competing for the social event of the season. The competition included hiring away their neighbor's yardmen, carpenters, and staff. Though polite face to face, there was a lot of hidden jealousy among the community's members.

Over the years a number of these mansions burned to the ground. Away from any fire-fighting companies, once a fire got started, it was common for the house to go up completely. Although many of the fire sources could be traced to something accidental, rumors were constantly swirling that some of the fires were set deliberately. It is easy to imagine how a family could get financially over-extended in such an environment, but there was at least one incident that went far beyond that.

There were two families on neighboring islands who started out being friends. The young couples traveled together, worked together, and built mansions on adjacent islands. For a time they took turn about throwing parties, entertaining friends and clients with a wide variety of activities. Then, almost overnight, the families had a falling out.

The rumor was that one of the men became involved with the other man's wife. Dividing the business associations and splitting the personal assets became much too complex, and would result in financial ruin for both parties. The problem was resolved quite handily when one of the mansions burned to the ground one night, trapping and killing the wayward man and his wife.

Although there were several areas of suspicion concerning the fire, the local authorities investigated and quickly declared it a tragic accident. Coincidentally, the local constable was soon building his own expensive new home, which did nothing to dispel rumors of a cover-up.

The beneficiary on the insurance policy covering the house turned out to be the business partner, the man living next door. This served to increase the whispers and gossip.

The surviving couple became much more reclusive and seldom entertained after that. In less than a year, their house also burned to the ground, and this time only the wife perished in the fire. Again, it was quickly ruled an accidental fire. The new widower sold the islands and wasn't heard from again. But that wasn't the end of the story.

A few months after the second fire, the local constable committed suicide, or at least that was the ruling. He was found sitting in his patrol car at the edge of the river, shot once in the head with his own revolver.

 People began reporting seeing a woman roaming the ruins of the burned mansions. Whenever anyone went to investigate, she would be gone, but would again be sighted shortly afterward. Even after the remains of the mansions were removed, the woman was still seen on the islands.

A banker from Philadelphia purchased one of the islands and built his own elaborate manor. His wife spent about two weeks at the home and moved out, refusing to spend another night. She claimed that she walked into a hallway and met a woman in a white evening dress. The woman looked distressed, and then faded into the woodwork.

The third time this happened was enough, and the lady left the island, vowing never to return. The house was vacant for about a month, and then burned to the ground.

THE LIGHTS IN BARNETT MARSH

Wellesley Island is one of the larger islands in the Thousand Islands chain. It is about halfway between Clayton and Alexandria Bay, and is a popular American

vacation site with its many boat docks and campsites. As with many of the islands, the population increases drastically during the summer season. It has two State Parks, a nature center, several golf courses, and the usual array of water sports to keep its visitors busy and entertained.

The parks include Wellesley Island State Park, Dewolf Point State Park, and Mary Island State Park, which isn't technically on Wellesley Island, but separated by a small channel.

Originally, the main function of the island was for farming. In the early 1900s George Boldt had a large farming enterprise on the island, using much of the farm's output of foods in his Waldorf Astoria Hotel in New York City.

Boating and fishing were also popular attractions, with Densmore Bay, Eel Bay, South Bay, and the Lake of the Isles, an inland lake on the island, drawing much attention.

There was another region on the island drawing attention, also, and it wasn't for its boating, fishing, or farming attributes. Barnett Marsh drew attention for a more mystifying reason.

There were occasional reports of strange lights being sighted in Barnett Marsh in the late 1800s, but these sightings intensified during the 1920s. People described the lights as round balls of fire moving slowly across the swamp. Usually the lights hovered a few feet off the surface, but occasionally they were reported to suddenly shoot straight upward, disappearing in the night sky.

Some people saw multiple lights, and thought the lights were moving in some type of unison. Others only saw a single light, and it barely moved at all before disappearing down into the marsh.

There were a number of theories to explain the lights. Of course there was the usual explanation of it being simply swamp gas, but that didn't explain some of the movements of the lights. Reflections from other sources were also used to justify the sightings, but nobody could explain exactly how that happened.

 Then in the late 1920s an event occurred which seemed to throw a different slant on the lights. Three men were hunting near the edge of the marsh late one night when they suddenly came upon a mysterious light. This was the closest that anyone had ever reported being to the light.

The men all agreed that it was more of a blue glow than an actual light, but that wasn't the strangest part. Within the glow was a face of a beautiful woman. She had long, straight hair and a hauntingly sad expression on her face. She seemed to stare back at the men for several minutes, as they stood motionless in shock.

One of the men finally found his voice and spoke to the apparition, asking who it was. Immediately the face closed its eyes, then the entity slowly moved in and out amidst the three men before sinking into the ground and disappearing.

While the apparition was between the men, they described how they could see through it, but could clearly see the face at the same time. As soon as it disappeared, the men decided that their hunting was over and quickly left the area. They didn't tell anyone of their experience for several days, fearing ridicule. When they did disclose what they had seen, however, it was met with more interest than disbelief.

Soon stories began cropping up attempting to explain this latest sighting. Some versions attributed the face to an Indian maiden who met an untimely end in the marsh. Other versions had the face tied to a young woman who lost her lover in the area, due to a shipwreck, duel, wild animal, or suicide.

In most versions the ghostly apparition was continuing to search for something; either a lost lover or not accepting her own sad fate. One explanation for there sometimes being several lights sighted was that it was the ghosts of a search party, hunting for the lost maiden.

The reported sightings of the lights dwindled away for a few decades, then in the 1980s reports again surfaced of there being an eerie light out in the marsh. Whatever is out there is referred to as the Strange Light in Barnett Marsh.

THE GHOSTS AT GANANOQUE INN

Island ownership in the Canadian part of the region began in the 1870s. Soon Tremont Park and Hay Island, located close to Gananoque, were popular vacation sites. With the influx of guest houses, also came industry. One of the earliest businesses in Gananoque was the Gananoque Carriage Works, founded by George and Charles Taylor.

The business was bought in 1885 by George Burrows of the Standard Wagon Company of Cincinnati, and later moved to Brockville. The pictorial location was not to go unused, however, and the property was soon converted into a summer hotel for the tourism industry.

The hotel was opened in 1896 under the operation of the Brockville Carriage Company. In 1906 the hotel was purchased by Archibald Welsh, who became the first private owner of the site.

Alas, a scant year later, in 1907, a fire destroyed much of the hotel. Without any hesitation, the owner quickly rebuilt the hotel, eager to reopen for the tourist season.

But rumors began to float around Gananoque that perhaps that ideal location for a hotel wasn't as perfect as it seemed. There were spirits who were troubled with the use of the land. They were not happy with the Gananoque Inn, or perhaps more accurately, the earlier tenant, the Gananoque Carriage Works.

According to legend, the Carriage Works was built on land that was in dispute. While the early owners insisted that they had purchased the land legally, there was an Indian version of the story that the land was never meant to be sold. It was home to an old Indian burial ground, specifically chosen for its aesthetic beauty, enabling the spirits to rest peacefully.

Although most folk scoff at the idea of a curse, there are stories that have been passed down over the generations that the Indians did not ever totally give up the land.

During the time the Carriage Works was operational, strange things occurred regularly. Workers would suddenly get violently ill, items would continually get misplaced, and there were several unexplained fires. There was a certain corner in one of the buildings that was noticeably colder than the rest of the building. Although it was passed off as being in a draft or some such, others insisted that the corner was haunted. Eventually the corner was walled off and only used for long-term storage.

Once the Gananoque Inn replaced the Carriage Works, it was hoped that the curse would be over. That wasn't the case, as the strange things continued happening, even before the Inn was completed. One of the workers began behaving in a quite crazy manner, mumbling in a confused Indian tongue that nobody could understand. Once he was removed from the construction site, he regained his normal senses. The worker refused to return to the work site, and would not discuss what brought on the spell he had been under.

The devastating fire at the Inn in 1907 also had a mystery surrounding it. The fire appeared to have started spontaneously, without any valid explanation.

Over the years there have also been ghosts or apparitions seen throughout the Inn. According to the legend, the burial grounds had been only for women and children, and the ghosts who have been reported follow that aspect.

A small Indian boy has been seen many times in the hallways, and several times people outside the Inn have seen him looking out a window. The boy seems bewildered by his surroundings and acts terrified of anyone who encounters him.

An Indian woman has been seen around a storage room near the back of the Inn many times. Sometimes she has seemed real, and at other times she has been semi-transparent. She never seems to be aware of anyone else around.

Although the sightings were frequent during the early 1900s, after the last major renovation there have been virtually no verified reports. Perhaps the Indian ghosts are at last at peace.

THE UNSPOKEN GHOST OF FORT HENRY

The Fort Henry National Historical Site is one of Kingston's premier historical attractions. It was originally built during the war of 1812, and a second version was constructed in the 1830s. It was abandoned in the late 1800s, but partially restored and used to house prisoners during World War I. Then it was abandoned, falling into much disrepair until 1936. Once again it was restored and opened as a museum in 1938.

Once a person enters the wooden gates of the fort today, it is like taking a step back into the 19th century. Visitors can watch the uniformed guards perform various military marches, see the changing of the guard ceremony, and witness an artillery attachment fire their guns.

The site is also known as a spooky 19th century fortress with some rather shocking history. There is an evening walking tour of the fort by lantern-light known as the "Ghosts of the Fort" outing. A cloaked tour guide will spin ghost tales along the way, intending to send shivers down the spines of the tourists. Among the stories told are those involving hangings at the courthouse, and the ghost of a pianist who continues to play. While this may

introduce the visitor to some of the fort's intrigue, there is another legend that will probably not be mentioned by the tour guides.

In the middle of the 19th century, there was an incident that rivaled the Jack-the-Ripper saga in old England. One morning a headless body was found floating in the river near the fort. The body was that of a young woman, and she not only was headless, but also armless. The theory was that the murderer cut off her arms and head to make her identification impossible.

A couple of weeks later, another body was found in the river. Again the body was headless and armless. This time, however, the authorities got a break. A tavern owner in Kingston reported that one of his waitresses failed to report to work, and that a search of her living quarters proved fruitless. In fact, this was the second waitress from his establishment who had suddenly disappeared recently.

A third body appeared a few weeks later, and the authorities linked her to another missing woman in Kingston. All of the victims had another thing in common, too. They were all prostitutes. They had all disappeared in the night, only to appear days later in the river, dismembered. One strange point was that the dismembering was performed using a very precise surgical method.

A month passed, and things settled down somewhat, but then another similar victim was found in the river. This tied in once again with a prostitute who had been reported missing a few days earlier.

There was panic throughout the red-light district in Kingston where the women had been working the streets and taverns. The police put extra men on the case, hoping to get some clues on the person victimizing the prostitutes.

All in all, there were seven known victims, all of them dismembered, all prostitutes, and all found floating in the river several days after they had disappeared. Then, as suddenly as it had started, the murderous episode stopped.

There was a story passed around that the murderer was probably sent to jail for some other crime, thus being taken out of circulation. Another suggestion was that the murderer had himself been killed. The police were happy to forget it and go on to other problems.

However, there was a more ominous rumor that circulated at the time; one involving Fort Henry. This rumor laid the blame for the murders on an officer at the fort. The victims had all disappeared coinciding with the officer being on leave and visiting Kingston. The man had private quarters, thus having the facility to keep a woman imprisoned for a couple of days. The officer was also a surgeon, with instruments available to do the dismembering. Finally, the killings stopped when this officer was suddenly transferred back to his home in England.

The rumor was that the man's superior officer discovered his guilt, and rather than have such a heinous crime associated with the fort, sent the man away, intending to let things blow over.

Things did not, however, settle down as quietly as the superior officer had hoped. A few months after the final victim had been found, a group of soldiers were returning to the fort late one night. Standing in front of the massive wooden gates was a lady dressed in a long white gown. The frightening thing was she had no head.

None of the terrified soldiers would approach the ghostly figure, but instead yelled for the guard inside the gate. When the gates were opened, the figure disappeared into the night air.

Since the soldiers had been drinking, nobody believed their story. Exactly one year later, however, a similar ghostly apparition was seen near the river bank. There were several witnesses, none had been drinking, and one was a high-ranking officer who nobody dared dispute. At that time the prior story began to be taken in a different light.

Supposedly this headless victim continues to make her appearance at the fort. She has been seen outside and inside the fort at various places, apparently continuing to haunt the location of her demise. Sometimes she appears armless as well as headless. This sinister spirit refuses to allow a gruesome history to die. Thus, now you've heard the story of the ghost that they don't talk about.

THE FRIENDLY GHOST OF CALUMET

George Emery made his fortune with the American Tobacco Company. He bought several islands in the Thousand Islands Region in the late 1800s, building elaborate summer homes for his family and for entertaining friends and business acquaintances.

In 1893-94 he culminated these structures with the Calumet Castle on Calumet Island. With over thirty rooms, a magnificent ballroom, and a cyclone cellar, the three-story castle was easily one of the more elaborate homes in the islands.

The spectacular Calumet Castle quickly became one of the most photographed structures around and helped to publicize the Thousand Islands Region. Its fame helped to inspire industry and other homes to be built in the area.

The castle stayed in the Emery family for several generations, with a trust fund set up to maintain it. Due to increasing taxes and costs of repairs, the upkeep on the property eventually outgrew the available funds left in the trust. After several unsuccessful attempts, the will was finally overturned by the courts, allowing the property to be sold in 1950.

The new owner did some remodeling and opened the castle as a tourist attraction. This endeavor did quite well for a few years, but then it caught fire and burned completely to the ground in 1957. Today a boating marina stands amidst the rubble remaining from the castle.

The rubble is not the only thing left from the glory days of Calumet Castle, however. It is also home to the mysterious Lady in Green.

Since the 1960s there have been reports of a lady in a green dress walking among the ruins of the castle. Although the reports have been sporadic, they have been quite consistent. The lady has long, wavy blonde hair and is sometimes wearing a pale yellow or straw hat. The hat has a green ribbon on it. She is occasionally carrying a parasol, twirling it as she walks along, or holding a bouquet of flowers. She has always been seen either in the early dawn or late in the afternoon, when the sunlight is somewhat subdued.

Not morose or mournful as are the ghosts in many reports, this lady seems to be quite happy. She is always smiling, and sometimes skips along as if propelled by sheer exhilaration. She is usually friendly, and has even been seen waving to passersby. She must have a shy side though, as she disappears into thin air whenever anyone gets close to her. Attempts to photograph her have always resulted in pictures without her in them, although there has been at least one picture showing a hazy mist where the lady had stood.

This friendly ghost has been reported at the castle ruins for decades, and a year never goes by without at least a couple of reported sightings. No one has come up with a sound theory of who the ghost might be, as she doesn't resemble any of the known family members who resided at the castle over the years. Perhaps she is simply the spirit of a lady who liked the castle.

THE GHOSTS OF CLAYTON

The Clayton area is considered to be the cultural center of the Thousand Islands Region. It has three outstanding museums, including the Antique Boat Museum which

claims to contain the finest collection of antique boats and engines in the world. This museum also hosts a number of activities, including boat rides in various types of craft and an antique show and auction. It even offers boat-building classes. Proud of its boating history, there are many boat tours to take visitors to various historical points of interest around Clayton.

There is also the Handweaving Museum and Arts Center, located in a historic village building, which has a variety of art instruction and exhibits. This museum hosts the Antique Show & Sale and the Annual Craft Show.

Clayton's third museum is the Thousand Islands Museum, famous for depictions of river life along the St. Lawrence Seaway, and has now opened an archival library, making available much river heritage to researchers.

Clayton is also well versed in the theatrical arts. It has a waterfront concert series each summer, and has a fabulous seasonal theatre in the village's restored opera house.

Museums and theatres are natural attractions for ghosts, and Clayton has its share of the supernatural, as well. The Clayton Opera House has seen entertainers from all over the world during its heyday, and a few of these performers apparently still lurk in the nooks and crannies of the theatre.

For many years, each spring when the staff began preparing the building for the upcoming season, inevitably someone would encounter a ghost known as Bashful Basil.

When a storeroom door was opened, the figure of a short, stout man would appear briefly among the stored items. He would act startled, then quickly disappear through a nearby wall, sink into the floor, or vaporize in a bluish cloud of smoke.

It was like Basil had spent the winter among the theatre props, and then immediately rushed from view when discovered. He might not be glimpsed again that season.

Another ghostly figure seen occasionally around the building was a young woman. She was generally sighted around the costume storage areas. If discovered, she usually had a scowl on her face, as if irritated at being interrupted. She, like Basil, would immediately disappear.

One story was that she was the ghost of a seamstress who worked there during the early days of the building's history. She seemed to be forever destined to hover

around the costumes, as if she felt a responsibility for their safety.

Another entity has been seen around the Opera House in more recent times. This ghost is often spotted when a production is about to open, as if he is checking out the quality of the show. He is a tall man, usually glimpsed in a back corner of the theatre. Some claim that he wears a long-tailed coat, and has white gloves, but most witnesses haven't gotten that close a view.

The museums of Clayton have not escaped their haunting residents, either. In the boat museum, apparitions are sometimes seen in the boats, as if part of a ghostly crew. These are seldom seen during the day, but workers in the museum at night have reported seeing these beings.

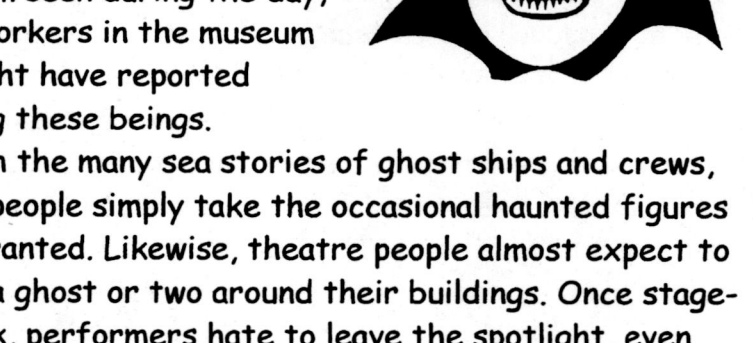

With the many sea stories of ghost ships and crews, boat people simply take the occasional haunted figures for granted. Likewise, theatre people almost expect to have a ghost or two around their buildings. Once stage-struck, performers hate to leave the spotlight, even after death.

THE PIRATE GHOSTS OF GOOSE BAY

Goose Bay and Cranberry Creek are located along the St. Lawrence River, about three miles northeast of Alexandria Bay. Goose Bay is a large, sheltered bay, containing several islands of various sizes. Much of this area is protected from prevailing winds and wave action, making it somewhat tranquil.

Cranberry Creek is a large stream which runs into the south end of Goose Bay. The creek's flow is seasonal, with little flow during the summer, but more during the winter months.

The surrounding area consists of marshland and forests. The wetlands have discouraged cabin development except around the hamlet of Goose Bay itself. Most of this land is privately owned, and is in a relatively undisturbed condition. At least it is for the most part. Sporadically it is invaded by fortune hunters, and legend has it that these interlopers are not received kindly.

Back in the 1800s there was a lot of pirate activity in this area. These scavengers of the sea preyed on the boat traffic sailing up and down the St. Lawrence River and nearby Lake Ontario. Goose Bay proved to be a convenient location for the pirates to hide, both themselves and their ill-gained treasure.

There are many stories concerning pirate loot buried around the islands and coves of Goose Bay. One of particular interest involves the feeder stream of Cranberry Creek.

During the dry summer months, Cranberry Creek sometimes dwindles to a trickle. During this dry season there are areas exposed which are beneath the water the rest of the year. There is supposed to be a large treasure buried a short distance up the Cranberry Creek that has been untouched by human hands for over a hundred and fifty years. At least it hasn't been touched by live humans.

A pirate gang had made several lucrative raids on the boating traffic along the river. This culminated with the capture of a load of gold coins on the way to Fort Henry. The pirate leader knew that the capture of the fort's payroll would generate a lot of interest, so he quickly sailed into Goose Bay, intent on finding a clever hiding place.

The spot chosen by the pirate was up in the Cranberry

Creek channel. The treasure was buried along the bank of the creek, and as was the custom, a couple of the pirate crew members were killed and buried with it. Their spirits were to guard the treasure.

Most of the pirate gang was killed by the military shortly thereafter. The leader escaped, and months later returned to Goose Bay eager to retrieve his treasure. Unfortunately this was during a wet winter and the area where the treasure had been hidden was completely underwater, and the main markings had been destroyed. The pirate returned several times, but was never able to find the spot where he had buried the loot. In a drunken stupor he eventually blurted out what he knew about the hiding spot, causing a flurry of hopeful treasure seekers to descend upon the area.

Immediately rumors began spreading up and down the river that the mouth of Cranberry Creek was haunted. Anyone venturing near the place was apt to find themselves at the mercy of savage pirate ghosts. Whether these rumors had factual roots, or whether they were simply spread in attempts to discourage treasure hunters is not clear.

One hunter was reported to have been found drifting in his boat in Goose Bay. He had been hacked to death by a large knife. Another treasure hunter was discovered on a small island near the creek, with his throat slashed. There have been accounts of several more victims, their deaths attributed to the spirits guarding the treasure.

According to the legend, many people passing near the creek have seen these large, menacing figures patrolling the area. These figures float along the ground and are able to move very quickly. They are armed with large knives, and will not allow anyone to pass by them.

The treasure is rumored to still be in its resting place, accessible only during the dry summer months, available to anyone brave enough to confront its protectors.

EPILOGUE

The Thousand Islands Region covers several miles of the St. Lawrence River. This expanse was occupied by various cultures going back many hundreds of years. It was populated by the earliest Indian tribes, and then traveled by some of the initial European explorers, who

 "discovered" its treasures and strategic location. Trappers and hunters, and later the lumber companies, found it bountiful with the means to satisfy their needs. Then, finally, people realized what a really picturesque area it was, and a great area for summer vacationers.

The region has a long and storied history, but the type of the history is what served our purpose. The river was traveled by ships, barges, pirates, and small crafts. Seafarers are some of the most superstitious people

around, and tales of lost ships, crews, and treasure are plentiful.

Proud of their history, settlers protected their heritage by stocking museums. Summer vacationers brought culture with them, establishing hotels, theatres, and opera houses. Performers are a very superstitious lot, and rare is a stage without its resident ghost.

Tragedy was common throughout the area, due to shipwrecks, pirates, war battles, and structures burning to the ground. All of these things spawn more ghosts, or at least ghost stories.

Along with the many Indians who roamed the region came numerous Indian legends. These legends frequently told of encounters with spirits, ghosts, and other supernatural entities.

Thus, there are probably more ghost stories connected with the Thousand Islands vicinity than any area comparable in size. Almost everything about the region connects easily to a haunting of some type. This book only taps the tip of the iceberg to the enormous wealth of ghost stories told about the Thousand Islands.

The author has not attempted to authenticate any of these stories, as it is the pure nature of ghost stories that they can't be proven or unproven. It is left to the listener, or reader, to decide for themselves what to believe and what to ignore. When you think about it, isn't almost everything somebody's imagination?

AUTHOR'S BIO

I was born and raised in Middle Tennessee, which is known for its abundance of creeks and lakes. The Tennessee River wasn't far from my home, either, with fishing and camping sites readily available to entice the weekend outdoorsmen.

But what really impressed me in my youth was my first visit to the Atlantic Ocean. It was at Daytona Beach, Florida, and I thought it was the most impressive and wonderfully awesome sight I had ever seen. In fact, I guess I still  think that. I marveled at its indescribable size and beauty, experiencing a kinship to nature one can only feel in the company of such spectacular views.

Thanks to this long affection with bodies of water, writing about the many scenic locations throughout the

Thousand Islands Region was quite enjoyable. I hope that my feeble attempts at describing the beauty of that area will entice the reader to visit that locale. You will not be disappointed.

If you are interested in what else has influenced my varied writings, please visit my website at:
www.larryhillhouse.com

GHOSTS OF INTERSTATE 90 Chicago to Boston by D. Latham

GHOSTS of the **Whitewater Valley** by Chuck Grimes

GHOSTS of Interstate 74   by B. Carlson

GHOSTS of the Ohio Lakeshore Counties by Karen Waltemire

GHOSTS of **Interstate 65**   by Joanna Foreman

GHOSTS of Interstate 25 by Bruce Carlson

GHOSTS of the Smoky Mountains by Larry Hillhouse

GHOSTS of the Illinois Canal System by David Youngquist

GHOSTS of the **Niagara River** by Bruce Carlson

Ghosts of Little Bavaria   by Kishe Wallace

Shown above (at 85% of actual size) are the spines of other Quixote Press books of ghost stories.
These are available at the retailer from whom this book was procured, or from our office at 1-800-571-2665 cost is $9.95 +
$3.50 S/H.

GHOSTS of Lookout Mountain by Larry Hillhouse

GHOSTS of Interstate 77 by Bruce Carlson

GHOSTS of Interstate 94 by B. Carlson

GHOSTS of MICHIGAN'S U. P. by Chris Shanley-Dillman

GHOSTS of the FOX RIVER VALLEY by D. Latham

GHOSTS ALONG I-35 by B. Carlson

Ghostly Tales of Lake Huron **by Roger H. Meyer**

Ghost Stories by Kids, for Kids by some really great fifth graders

Ghosts of Door County Wisconsin by Geri Rider

Ghosts of the Ozarks *B Carlson*

Ghosts of US - 63 by Bruce Carlson

Ghostly Tales of Lake Erie by Jo Lela Pope Kimber

Ghosts of Interstate 75	by Bruce Carlson
Ghosts of Lake Michigan	by Ophelia Julien
Ghosts of I-10	by C. J. Mouser
GHOSTS OF INTERSTATE 55	by Bruce Carlson
Ghosts of US - 13, Wisconsin Dells to Superior	by Bruce Carlson
Ghosts of I-80	David youngquist
Ghosts of Interstate 95	by Bruce Carlson
Ghosts of US 550	by Richard DeVore
Ghosts of Erie Canal	by Tony Gerst
Ghosts of the Ohio River	by Bruce Carlson
Ghosts of Warren County	by Various Writers
Ghosts of I-71 Louisville, KY to Cleveland,OH	by Bruce Carlson

GHOSTS OF DALLAS COUNTY	by Lori Pielak
Ghosts of US - 66 from Chicgo to Oklahoma	By McCarty & Wilson
Ghosts of the Appalachian Trail	by Dr. Tirstan Perry
Ghosts of I- 70	by B. Carlson
Ghosts of the Thousand Islands	by Larry Hillhouse
Ghosts of US - 23 in Michigan	by B. Carlson
Ghosts of Lake Superior	by Enid Cleaves
GHOSTS OF THE IOWA GREAT LAKES	by Bruce Carlson
Ghosts of the Amana Colonies	by Lori Erickson
Ghosts of Lee County, Iowa	by Bruce Carlson
The Best of the Mississippi River Ghosts	by Bruce Carlson
Ghosts of Polk County Iowa	by Tom Welch

Ghosts of Ohio's Lake Erie shores & Islands Vacationland by B. Carlson

Ghosts of Des Moines County   by Bruce Carlson

Ghosts of the Wabash River   by Bruce Carlson

Ghosts of Michigan's US 127   by Bruce Carlson

GHOSTS OF I-79   *BY BRUCE CARLSON*

Ghosts of US-66 from Ft. Smith to Flagstaff   by Connie Wilson

Ghosts of US 6 in Pennslyvania   by Bruce Carlson

Ghosts of the Lower Missouri   by Marcia Schwartz

Ghosts of the Tennessee River in Tennessee   by Bruce Carlson

Ghosts of the Tennessee River in Alabama

Ghosts of Michigan's US 12 by R. Rademacher & B. Carlson

Ghosts of the Upper Savannah River from Augusta to Lake Hartwell   by Bruce Carlson

Mysteries of the Lake of the Ozarks   Hean & Sugar Hardin

To Order Copies

Please send me _____ copies of *Ghosts of 1000 Islands* at $9.95 each plus $3.50 S/H. (Make checks payable to Quixote Press.)

Name _____

Street _____

City _____ State _____ Zip _____

QUIXOTE PRESS
3544 Blakslee Street
Wever IA   52658
1-800-571-2665

To Order Copies

Please send me _____ copies of *Ghosts of 1000 Islands* at $9.95 each plus $3.50 S/H. (Make checks payable to Quixote Press.)

Name _____

Street _____

City _____ State _____ Zip _____

QUIXOTE PRESS
3544 Blakslee Street
Wever IA   52658
1-800-571-2665